DATE DUE			
AUG 8 1989			
SEP 8 1990			
AUG 2 2 1990			
AUG 9 1991			
AUG 2 2 1991			
OCT 2 1 1992			
JAN 3 0 '04			

LIFE WITH MAX

Care

Copyright © 1989 American Teacher Publications
Published by Raintree Publishers Limited Partnership
Library of Congress number: 89-3605

Library of Congress Cataloging in Publication Data

Carlson, Judy.
  Life with Max / Judy Carlson; illustrated by Pat Hoggan.

  (Real readers)
  Summary: A big sister has trouble coping with her young brother.
  [1. Brothers and sisters—Fiction.] I. Hoggan, Pat, ill. II. Title. III. Series.
PZ7.C216626Li 1989   [E]—dc19   89-3605
ISBN: 0-8172-3525-6

1 2 3 4 5 6 7 8 9 0   93 92 91 90 89

REAL READERS

LIFE WITH MAX

by Judy Carlson
illustrated by Pat Hoggan

Raintree Publishers
Milwaukee

Do you think it's easy being a big sister? Well, it's not! I am seven. Max is five. He really knows how to make me mad.

Little things, big things. Max knows what gets me mad.

Do you want to know what he does? Well, when I play the piano, where do you think Max plays with his trucks? Yes, right under the piano! How can I play sweet, pretty songs with CRASH, SMASH, CRUSH, under my feet?

So I do what I always do when I get mad at Max. My face gets red, and I shout, "MAAAXXX!"

He just thinks that's funny.

Last week, I went into my bedroom. I didn't see any of my stuffed animals there. Then I went to find Max. He was in the bathroom. The tub was filled to the top with water. He had put all of my animals into the tub! He said he was teaching them how to swim!

ARGH! Do you know how long it takes stuffed animals to dry?

MAAAXXX!

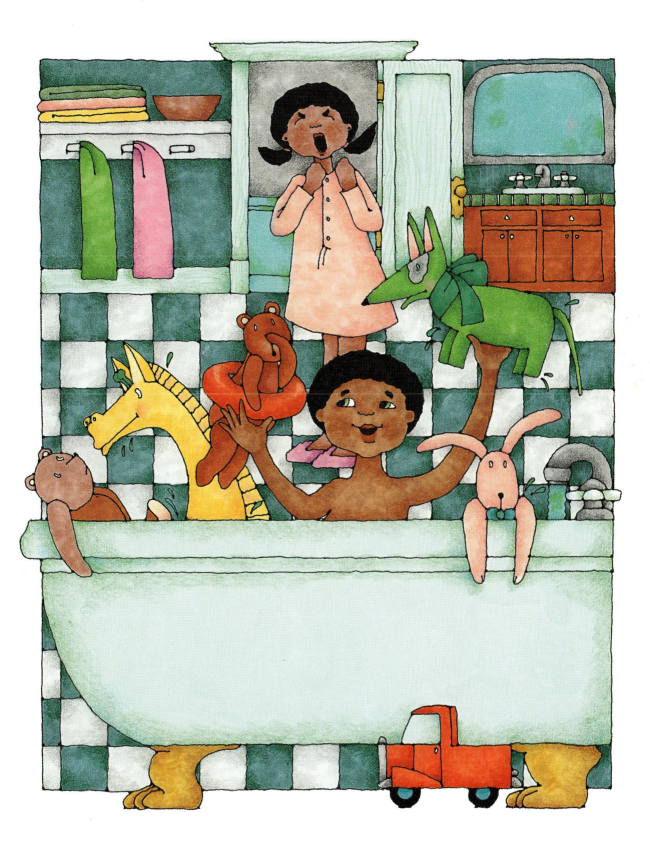

After that, I had had it with Max. "I have to stop him," I thought. "But how?"

Then I got an idea. "I will bug him!" I thought.

So I waited. Then one night Max had just turned on the TV show he liked most. I ran in front of the TV set. I began singing and jumping up and down.

Did Max cry? Did he yell at me to stop bugging him? NO! He laughed and started singing and jumping with me!

ARGH! See? He really knows how to make me mad!

My next idea was to tell Mom and Dad every time Max bugged me.

Last night he said he was the Wind. Then he started blowing my baseball cards all over the room. I shouted, "MAAAXXX!" And then I shouted, "MOM! DAD! MAKE HIM STOP!"

"He's just little," said Dad.

"He'll help you pick them up," said Mom.

Ha! Knowing Max, he would <u>eat</u> them before he would pick them up! Mom and Dad were no help at all.

Today I got a new idea. I would get away from Max and stay away from him. I put a sign on my door that said, "STAY OUT MAX." He doesn't know how to read, but he got the idea. Then I took all my stuff into my room.

"I want to come in too," said Max.

"Never," I said.

"Please?" he said.

"Ha!" I said. Then I closed the door.

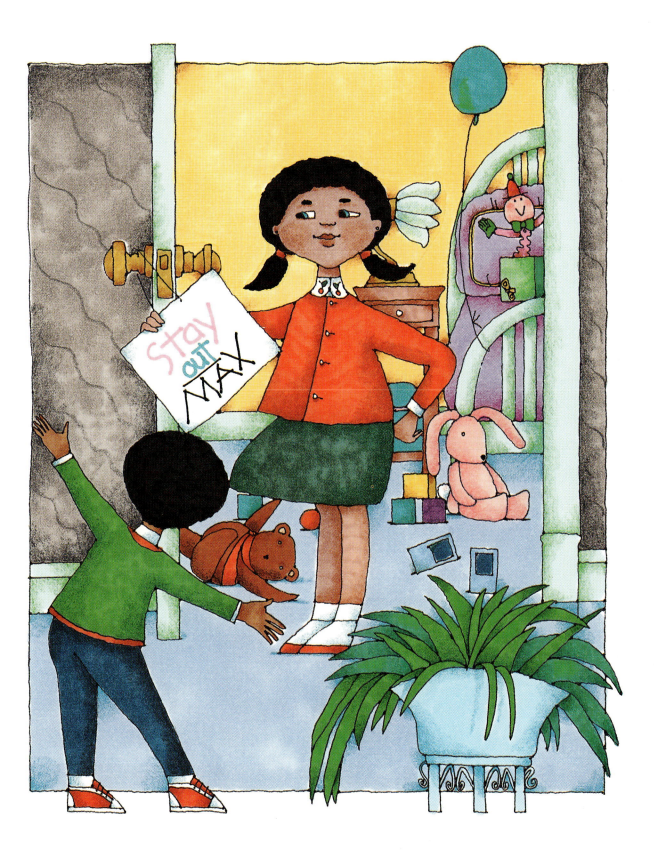

Ah, it was so nice. No Max! "This is the life," I thought. "No fighting, no yelling. Nothing but peace and quiet."

I took out my baseball cards and stacked them by teams. I played with all of my stuffed animals. I made a big elephant out of clay.

But —

But —

Something wasn't right.

It was too — too — quiet. The funny thing was that I missed Max!

I opened my bedroom door. Max was standing out in the hall. He looked very sad.

So do you know what I did? I shouted, "MAAAXXX!"

He looked up.

"Come on in and bug me," I said.

I guess being Max's big sister isn't _so_ bad.

Oh no! Time to go! Max is starting to drop my baseball cards out the window.

MAAAXXXXXXXXXXXXXXXXXXXXXXX!

Sharing the Joy of Reading

Beginning readers enjoy reading books on their own. Reading a book is a worthwhile activity in and of itself for a young reader. However, a child's reading can be even more rewarding if it is shared. This sharing can enhance your child's appreciation — both of the book and of his or her own abilities.

Now that your child has read **Life with Max**, you can help extend your child's reading experience by encouraging him or her to:

- Retell the story or key concepts presented in this story in his or her own words. The retelling can be oral or written.

- Create a picture of a favorite character, event, or concept from this book.

- Express his or her own ideas and feelings about the characters in this book and other things the characters might do.

Here is an activity that you can do together to help extend your child's appreciation of this book: You and your child can share some happy or funny memories about family members. Tell your child a story that you remember about him or her, or about some other family member. Encourage your child to tell you a happy story or memory that he or she has about a family member. You might want to pull out photographs to use as a starting point for discussing your family stories and memories.